MARTHA SPEAKS

Fireworks for All

Adaptation by Karen Barss
Based on a TV series teleplay written by Dietrich Smith

Based on the characters created by Susan Meddaugh

HOUGHTON MIFFLIN HARCOURT
Boston · New York

Ages 5–7 • Grade: 2
Guided Reading Level: J
Reading Recovery Level: 17

For information about permission to reproduce selections from this book, write to Permissions, Houghton Mifflin Harcourt Publishing Company, 215 Park Avenue South, New York, New York 10003.

Library of Congress Cataloging-in-Publication Data is on file.

ISBN 978-0-547-42892-5 pb | ISBN 978-0-547-42897-0 hc

Design by Rachel Newborn

www.hmhbooks.com
www.marthathetalkingdog.com

Manufactured in Singapore / TWP 10 9 8 7 6 5 4 3 2
4500273811

Hooray!
School is out for the summer!

"What do you love most about summer?"
asks Helen.
"No school!" says T.D.
"No school, and ice cream!" says Alice.

"And every Saturday night," says Helen,
". . . *fireworks!*"

"They start next Saturday," Truman says.
Martha begins to worry.

"I think fireworks
are kind of scary,"
Martha says.
"Scary? No way!"
Helen replies.

Later, Helen's family eats dinner.
Mom asks, "Did you hear that
Mrs. Demson wants to ban fireworks?
Her goal is to have many people sign
the ban."

"If you ban fireworks, do you stop them?"
asks Martha.
"Yes," says Helen. "That would be too bad."

Martha meets her friends.
They are all very sad.
Fireworks are scary to dogs.

Ruff, woof, growl!

"Fireworks are too loud," Martha agrees. "But there is something we can do to stop them."

The dogs go to the park.
"We want to help ban fireworks," Martha
tells Mrs. Demson.

But Mrs. Demson does not like dogs.
"Go away! Shoo!" she says.

"I have another plan," Martha tells her friends.
"I can talk. I will ask people to sign the ban."

At the park, people sign their names.
Mrs. Demson is happy.
So is Martha.

"That's it," says Mrs. Demson at the end
of the day.
"No more fireworks!"

"No more fireworks?" says Helen.
She rushes to tell her friends.

Martha meets the gang.
"Hi," she says. "What's up?"
"Nothing," T.D. says.
"Summer is ruined, that's all."

Martha looks at the poster.
"I am sorry, but fireworks are really scary
for dogs."

Helen asks, "Scary? Really?"
"I tried to tell you," says Martha.
"They are too loud."

"Martha, I'm so sorry I did not listen,"
Helen says.
"I have an idea that can save the fireworks
and your ears."

"You can watch *Courageous Collie Carlo* shows at the movie theater," says Helen.
"You won't hear the fireworks."

"A special evening show just for dogs!"
says Martha.
"Every dog in town will be there!"